STORIES FROM
THE BIBLE

Old Testament Stories Retold

by MARTIN WADDELL

illustrated by GEOFFREY PATTERSON

TICKNOR & FIELDS

New York • 1993

For Isobel —M.W.

For Roberta Reynolds —G.P.

First American edition 1993 published by Ticknor & Fields,
A Houghton Mifflin company, 215 Park Avenue South,
New York, New York 10003

First published in Great Britain by Frances Lincoln Limited,
Apollo Works, 5 Charlton Kings Road, London NW5 2SB.
All rights reserved. For information about permission to
reproduce selections from this book, write to Ticknor & Fields,
215 Park Avenue South, New York, New York 10003.

Manufactured in Hong Kong

ISBN 0-395-66902-2
Text of this book is set in ITC Garamond Book
The illustrations are acrylic paintings

10 9 8 7 6 5 4 3 2 1

Library of Congress Cataloging-in-Publication Data

Waddell, Martin.
Stories from the Bible : Old Testament stories retold / by Martin
Waddell ; illustrated by Geoffrey Patterson. — 1st American ed.
p.   cm.
Summary: A collection of Bible stories from the Old Testament,
from the Creation to the adventure of Jonah.
ISBN 0-395-66902-2
1. Bible stories, English—O.T.   [1. Bible stories—O.T.]
I. Patterson, Geoffrey, ill.   II. Title.
BS551.2.W2185   1993
221.9'505—dc20   92-36114   CIP   AC

Contents

About these stories

The Bible is the source of these stories.

The early Scriptures relate the history of the relationship between God and His chosen people, the Jews, descendants of Abraham, Isaac, and Jacob. They contain many details of theological and ritual significance which are beyond the grasp of children.

I write for children, not theologians, and my aim in selecting and freely adapting these stories has been to make them more accessible to children, while remaining true to my own understanding of the original. Inevitably, this gives rise to problems of interpretation.

These stories should be read with the Bible, and not instead of it.

The Creation

his story begins with God. It has to, because before there was anything else at all, there was God.

God said: "Let there be light!"

And there was.

It was great. God was pleased. He separated the light from the darkness, and He called the light *day* and the darkness *night*, and there was morning and evening, the very first day.

The next day God made Heaven and Earth, doing the big things first.

On the third day God made the seas and the land, and when He had finished doing that He made all the things that grow on the land — grass and flowers and trees, everything! He made each thing with seeds, like the seeds in an apple or the middle of a daisy, so that when one plant withered and died another would replace it.

On the fourth day, He made the sun and the moon and the stars, working on the big things again. He made the sun for the day, and the moon for the night. He was pleased with what He had done.

The next day, the fifth one, He got busy with the details. He made all the birds in the sky and the fish in the sea. He made them like the plants, with seeds inside them, so that they could have baby birds and baby fish, and there would always be birds and fish.

God was even busier on the sixth day, because that is when He made all the cows and horses and sheep and goats and camels and elephants and tigers and spiders and beetles and snails. He made everything that walks and everything that crawls or hops or slithers, and last of all

He made a man and a woman. He told the man and the woman that He had made the world for them, and they were to look after it. They had to care for the birds and fish and the plants and animals and insects and the world He had made for them, which had everything in it that they would ever need.

God rested on the seventh day, enjoying all that He had made.

It was perfect, beautiful, and wonderful.

Only God could have done it.

Adam and Eve

The first people God made were a man called Adam and a woman called Eve. This story is about what happened to them.

God made Adam from the dust of the earth. He breathed life into Adam, so that Adam became the first person on Earth.

Adam had to live somewhere, so God made a lovely garden, called Eden. It was filled with trees and flowers and fruit, with clear water running through it.

God brought all the other living things to Adam, and Adam gave them names. That is how a cow came to be called a cow, and a camel to be called a camel. There were many kinds of animals around by the time the name-giving had finished, but they were not good company for Adam. God thought about this and decided to make a woman, to be Adam's wife. First He put Adam into a deep sleep, and then He took one of Adam's ribs and made Eve from it, so that in an odd way they were one person. God made them to be together.

Adam and Eve had no clothes, but they didn't mind that, because it was the way God had made them, and they trusted God to get it right. They were like two innocent children in the beautiful garden, enjoying themselves with all the things God had made for them.

It didn't last.

There was a snake in the garden, who was more crafty and cunning than the other animals. The snake asked Eve what God had said about eating the things that grew in the garden.

"God said we could eat the fruit from the trees," Eve said, "but not the fruit from the tree in the middle of the garden. We are not allowed to eat it or touch it, and if we do, we'll die."

"You won't die," the snake said scornfully. "If you eat the fruit from that tree, you will be like God, and know everything. Go on, take a bite and see."

Eve believed the snake, and took a bite.

It was nice.

"You have a bite," Eve said to Adam. And Adam did, and they didn't die.

That started them thinking. If they didn't trust God in one thing, why should they trust Him in another? What about having no clothes, for instance? They felt ashamed at having no clothes on, and so they ran off and made some.

God came in the cool of the evening, walking in the garden.

Adam and Eve were frightened because they knew that they had disobeyed God, so they hid, which was no use at all. No one can hide from God.

God knew what they'd been up to.

There was a big argument.

Adam blamed Eve for giving him the fruit to eat, and Eve blamed the snake for suggesting it in the first place.

God was very angry with the snake. He told it that it would be the enemy of everything that lives on Earth. It would crawl on the ground and bite people and animals, and they would try to kill it when they saw it. So that took care of the snake.

God was unhappy that Adam and Eve had disobeyed Him. He told them that because they had eaten the fruit they would have to leave the beautiful garden and go out in the world to fend for themselves.

It was very sad, but it was their own fault for believing the snake and not putting their trust in God.

Noah and the Dove

Adam and Eve were very unhappy at being cast out of the garden, but things seemed to go well at first.

Eve had many babies.

The babies grew up and had babies, and their babies had babies, and the babies' babies had babies. This went on for hundreds of years. Soon there were people everywhere, but they kept fighting and quarrelling with each other, because they had forgotten how to be good.

God was very sad, but He saw that there was one good person left, a man called Noah. Noah wasn't like the others, fighting and quarrelling. He put his trust in God.

That is why God picked him out.

God told Noah that He was so sad at the way things had turned out that He was going to send a big flood to wash all the bad people away, and begin all over again, with just Noah and his family.

Noah thought that the flood might wash him away too, but God had it all worked out so that Noah would be saved. He told Noah to build an ark, which is a very big boat, and to put all his family in it, together with some of every kind of bird or animal or insect that lived on Earth. Noah was to put loads of food on the boat, enough food of different kinds for all of them to eat.

It may have seemed simple enough to God who can do anything, but it was a huge job for poor Noah.

Noah did it!

His wife helped, and so did his three sons, Shem and Ham and Japheth, and their wives. It took an enormous amount of work.

When all the work was finished, and the ark was filled up with birds and animals and insects and people and food, the rain started.

It began with just a drip-drip-drip, a few drops of rain.

"Hold tight everybody!" Noah said. "Close the door and shut the windows!"

The drips became pings and the pings became pongs and the pongs became plops and the plops became gushes and the wind roared and the heavens opened and . . .

WHOOOOOOOOSH!

The Flood!

It rained and it rained and it rained for forty days and forty nights, and the water rose and rose until the ark floated on top of it. Soon the water covered everything, even the tips of the tallest mountains, by which time all the living things that weren't in Noah's ark had been washed away and drowned. Some of the creatures that were in the ark were frightened, but not Noah.

Noah kept his trust in God.

God hadn't forgotten Noah either.

God made the rain stop, and He sent a wind to blow over the Earth and dry up the waters. The water started to go down.

On the seventeenth day of the seventh month . . .

BUMP!

The ark settled on the top of Mount Ararat, which was a very high mountain indeed.

There still was water everywhere.

It took three months before the tops of the other mountains were free of the water. Noah and his family and everything else had to stay in the ark all that time. They

were grumbly and impatient, stuck in a boat on top of a mountain with water all around them.

"Come on, Noah!" somebody would say. "We're sick of this! We want to get out of this old boat."

"You'll just have to wait," Noah said.

And they did.

They waited forty days, and then Noah sent a raven out to see if there was anywhere safe it could land. But there wasn't. The raven flew off and was never seen again.

Noah tried again, with a dove. The water was going down, but there still was sticky mud everywhere, and the dove couldn't find anywhere safe enough to land, so it flew back to the ark.

More grumbles!

"Wait!" Noah said.

They waited another seven days, and then Noah tried again.

This time, the dove came back with a freshly picked olive leaf, which meant that things were growing again and there was dry land to stand on.

"Off we go!" the people cheered. The animals and birds and insects couldn't cheer, but they were just as excited as Noah's family.

"Not yet!" said cautious Noah. He wasn't going to let anyone leap off the ark and skid down a muddy mountain into a puddle. He wanted to be sure everything and everybody would be safe, just as God had intended.

Noah waited another seven days, despite all the grumbling and excitement, and then he sent the dove off again.

This time, the dove didn't come back.

"Hooray!" the family shouted, and Noah let them all off the boat—his family, and every living thing that had been on the ark, so that God could help them to begin again.

The very first thing that Noah did when he got off the mountain was to build an altar to worship God.

God was very pleased.

God said to Noah, "I give you My word. Never again will there be a flood to destroy the Earth. I have set a rainbow in the clouds, and it will be the sign of My word. When a rainbow appears, I will remember My promise."

God blessed Noah and his family, and sent them out to fill the world with people.

The next story happened a long time later, to Abraham, who was a descendant of Noah's son Shem.

Abraham and Sarah

God loved the People, and He chose Abraham to lead them. He told Abraham to leave his father Terah's home and travel into the land of the Canaanites, who were descended from another of Noah's sons, Ham.

Abraham was seventy-five years old when he left Haran, the place where he had been living, and travelled into Canaan with his wife, Sarah, and his servants and his nephew.

Of course, when they got there, the land was full of Canaanites, but God promised Abraham: "One day this country will belong to your descendants."

"I don't have any children!" Abraham said. "If I have no children, I won't have any descendants!"

"Look at the sky," God said.

"I'm looking," Abraham said.

"Try counting the stars," God said. "You will have as many descendants as that."

There were so many stars that Abraham couldn't count them all.

A long time went by. Abraham was ninety-nine years old, and Sarah was eighty-nine, and still they had no child.

God spoke to Abraham again.

"I will bless your wife, Sarah, and I will give you a son by her," God said. "You will name your son Isaac. The promise I have made to you, I will keep with him and his children and their descendants. There will be kings among them, and this land will belong to them one day."

Abraham didn't doubt God, but still nothing happened, until one hot day three men came to the door of his tent.

Abraham went out to make them welcome. He had food and drink fetched for them, and they sat under a tree where he served them himself.

They asked him where his wife Sarah was.

"She's in the tent," Abraham said.

One of the men said: "Nine months from now, I will come back, and your wife Sarah will have a son."

Sarah was behind him, at the door of the tent, and she heard what the man said.

"I'm too old and worn out to have a baby!" she said. "So is Abraham!" And she laughed inside herself at the idea of two old people having a baby.

Then the man spoke again, and this time Abraham knew that he spoke with the voice of God.

"Why did Sarah laugh?" God asked. "Is anything too difficult for God? As I said, nine months from now I will return and Sarah will have a son."

"I didn't laugh!" Sarah said, because she was afraid that she had annoyed God.

"Oh, yes, you did!" God said. "You laughed!"

Nine months later she really had something to laugh about, because the baby Isaac was born, and Abraham and Sarah were laughing with joy!

In the language Abraham and Sarah spoke, the name Isaac means "He laughs."

Sarah said: "God has brought me joy and laughter. Everyone who hears about it will laugh with me!"

An old man of a hundred and a ninety-year-old woman, laughing and loving their tiny baby boy and thanking God for sending him to them . . . I think this is a lovely, happy, laughing story!

It is important, as well.

God had chosen Abraham to be the father of His people, and teach them to obey God and live good lives. If the people obeyed God, the promises God had made to Abraham would all come to pass.

Isaac, the child they called *He laughs*, would have children. There would be many hard times, and they would have to leave Canaan. They would become slaves in a strange country, but one day the descendants of Abraham and Isaac would return to the land God had promised them, if they put their trust in God.

The next story tells how God helped Abraham to find Isaac a wife.

Isaac and Rebecca

Abraham and Sarah loved their baby boy Isaac, and watched him grow to be a man. But they grew older too, and when Sarah was a hundred and twenty-seven years old, she died.

Isaac was terribly sad.

Abraham wanted to help his son, and he thought that the best thing to do would be to find Isaac a wife who would comfort him. He wanted Isaac's wife to be one of his own people, and not one of the people of Canaan, who did not believe in the one true God.

Abraham asked his oldest servant to go back to the land they had come from and find Isaac a wife from among his own people.

"What if she won't come?" the servant asked. "Will I send your son to her?"

"God has promised me that He will find a wife for Isaac who will be willing to come," Abraham said.

The servant went off with ten camels, and he journeyed until he came to the city where Abraham's brother Nahor lived.

He was in the right place, but he had no idea how to find the right girl! He didn't know what to do, so he knelt and prayed to God, for he knew that God had promised to help Abraham.

"God, keep Your promise to my master," the servant prayed.

Then he went to the well outside the city, because he knew that that was where the young women came to fetch water. They had to go to the well, because there wasn't much plumbing in those days, even in cities.

Just as he had expected, there were many women at the well. Big ones and small ones and fat ones and thin ones and ones with nice eyes or nice hair or pimples and ones who were quiet and ones who giggled all the time.

"How do I pick one?" Abraham's servant wondered again, and then he remembered that it wasn't up to him to choose. God was going to do it, because that is what God had promised Abraham.

What the servant needed was a special sign from God, and he stood there wondering what it could possibly be, because he didn't want to make a mistake. It had to be something extraordinary that would make one girl stand out from all the rest.

Then he thought: *Camels!*

Ten camels can drink a huge amount of water—jars and jars and jars of it.

The jars were big, and filling them was very hard work. Anyone who would give her water to the ten camels, filling up her jar again and again and again, would have to be extra special.

So the servant prayed to God and said, "I will ask one of the girls for a drink from her jar. If she says yes, and also gives me water for my ten camels, then I will know that she is the one You have chosen to be Isaac's wife, as You promised my master."

That is exactly what happened.

The girl's name was Rebecca. I don't know whether she was big or small or fat or thin or had nice hair or nice eyes or pimples or whether she was quiet or whether she giggled. God wouldn't bother about nice eyes or pimples or giggling, just about what she was like inside, because that is what matters to God.

That is how God kept His promise to Abraham and found a wife for Isaac, to help him get over his sadness at the death of his mother, Sarah.

Isaac and Rebecca married and had children, twin boys called Esau and Jacob. God gave Jacob a special name, which was *Israel*, and from then on the People of God were also called the Children of Israel.

The next story is about Jacob's son Joseph.

Joseph the Dreamer

Joseph was Jacob's youngest son-but-one. Jacob had a very big family, with twelve sons. The others were: Reuben, Simeon, Levi, Judah, Issachar, Zebulun, Benjamin, Dan, Naphtali, Gad, and Asher.

Joseph was his favorite.

It was "Joseph says this" or "Joseph does that" all day long, and the rest of the brothers got tired of hearing how wonderful Joseph was and how much Jacob loved him.

When Joseph was seventeen, Jacob made him a coat of many beautiful colors: red, green, blue, amber, pink, orange—all the colors you can think of. It was the sort of coat no one could help noticing, and Joseph went strutting around in it.

"Showoff!" his brothers thought.

Joseph started having strange dreams, and he told people about them. In one dream, Joseph and his brothers were in the fields, and the brothers' sheaves of wheat bowed down to Joseph's. In another, the sun and moon and stars bowed down to him, as if he were a king or something.

"This boasting has got to stop!" Jacob told Joseph. "What kind of a dream is that? Do you think that your mother, your brothers, and I are going to come and bow down to you?"

That is what Jacob said, but inside himself he was thinking deeply.

Suppose God was sending the dreams to Joseph? God must have a reason for doing it. What could the reason be?

Jacob was right, God *was* sending the dreams, and for a very strange reason, which nobody understood until a long time afterward.

Joseph's brothers went on grumbling about him, and Joseph went on swaggering about in his coat and letting everyone see that he was his father's favorite, and in the end the brothers found their chance to do something about it.

They were a long way from home, and Jacob had sent Joseph out in his beautiful coat to find them. They saw him coming – they could hardly miss him, dressed up like that in the middle of a field – and one of them said, "Here comes the Dreamer! Let's kill him and throw him into one of the old dried-up wells where no one will find him. We can tell father that a wild animal ate him. Then we'll see what becomes of his big dreams."

All the brothers agreed, except Reuben. He thought of a way to save Joseph, without the jealous brothers realizing what he was doing.

"Don't kill him," Reuben pleaded. "Just throw him down the well."

It sounded all right to the brothers, but what they didn't know was that Reuben planned to come back and get Joseph out of the well afterward, which was pretty smart of Reuben.

Poor Joseph!

They threw him down the well, but they ripped off his fancy coat first, because they planned to use it to convince Jacob that Joseph had been killed by a wild animal. It was a good thing that the well was dry, or Joseph would have drowned.

Away went the brothers with the coat, leaving Joseph stuck in the well.

Then one of the brothers, Judah, had a better idea.

"Why let Joseph die in the well?" Judah said. "We could make some money by selling him instead!"

Some of them went back and pulled Joseph up out of the well and sold him for twenty pieces of silver to a band of traders who were on their way to Egypt.

Reuben didn't know what they had done. He went back to the well.

No Joseph!

Poor Reuben! He had never meant to harm his brother, and now he had no idea what he was going to tell his father when he got home.

The other brothers took care of that. They killed a goat, and dipped Joseph's torn coat in its blood. Then they took the coat to Jacob and said, "We found this coat. Does it belong to anybody you know?"

It was a very cruel thing to do.

This time it was poor Jacob.

He believed that his favorite son had been killed. He cried and cried.

"I will die still mourning my son!" he groaned.

Everybody in the family tried to comfort him, but nobody could help, least of all the brothers. They knew what had really happened, but they couldn't tell their father the truth.

What they didn't know was that God had chosen Joseph to be a leader of His people. The strange dreams were a part of that, and so was going to Egypt.

God was watching over His people.

The next story tells what happened to Joseph in Egypt and why God wanted him to go there.

Joseph in Egypt

oseph went to Egypt as a slave, which was a bad beginning, but he did well. Then someone told lies about him, and he ended up in a smelly dungeon belonging to the King of Egypt, who was called the Pharaoh, feeling anything but rich and powerful.

God had used dreams before to change Joseph's life and He did it again. He had given Joseph the power to understand dreams, and the Pharaoh started having strange dreams.

"Get Joseph up here!" the Pharaoh said, and that got Joseph out of the dungeon.

This was one of the Pharaoh's dreams.

He dreamed that he was standing on the banks of the Nile, the big river that flows through Egypt. Seven fat cows came out of the river and began feeding in the grass. Then seven thin cows came, and they ate the fat ones, munching them up like big hamburgers without the bun. That was the first dream. The second was almost the same, but it was about seven thin stalks of corn eating up seven fat ones.

Joseph knew what the dreams meant. He told the Pharaoh that there would be seven years of great plenty in Egypt, followed by seven years of famine and starvation, with nothing growing on the land that could be eaten.

Then he told the Pharaoh what to do about it.

Joseph's idea was that they should store up all the corn they could during the seven good years, and then they would be able to use it to keep the people of Egypt from starving in the bad years.

The Pharaoh was so impressed that he made Joseph

Governor over all Egypt, so Joseph became a rich and important man, just as God intended.

The seven bad years didn't just happen in Egypt. They happened in Canaan too, where the Children of Israel were. Jacob didn't know what to do, but he heard that there was corn in Egypt, and he sent ten of the brothers to try and buy some from the clever Governor who had stored up corn in the good years. Jacob didn't send Benjamin, the youngest brother, because he had been frightened by losing Joseph. He wanted to make sure that he still had one son left, even if something terrible happened to the others.

Off went the brothers to buy corn from the Governor of all Egypt, but of course they didn't know who the Governor really was, and they didn't recognize him.

Joseph didn't tell his brothers who he was, although he recognized them.

He pretended that he didn't speak their language, and he seemed such an important and splendid person that he scared them.

Then he told them that he thought they were spies, which really made their knees knock.

"Oh, no, we're not!" they said.

"Oh, yes, you are," said Joseph, and he told them he was going to test them. He said he would give them the corn they wanted to take to their father and the others starving back in Canaan, but one of the brothers, Simeon, was to stay in prison in Egypt. The others could go back to Canaan with the corn, but they were to come back bringing their brother Benjamin with them. That would prove that the story they had told about their family starving was true.

The brothers had to agree.

They said to each other, "This has happened to us because of the way we treated Joseph."

"I pleaded with you not to hurt him," Reuben said. "You wouldn't listen to me, and now we are being punished."

Joseph still didn't let them know that he could understand what they were saying. He was making them suffer for a reason. He wanted to be sure that they were sorry for what they had done, and not just sorry for themselves. He sent them back to Canaan, but not before he had arranged another test.

When they got home, they opened the sacks of grain. The money that they had given the great Governor to pay

for the grain was in the sacks with it.

They were very frightened.

"The Governor will think we have cheated him!" they moaned. They were terrified, and they didn't know what to do. If they didn't go back, Simeon would be left a prisoner. If they did, they would have to take Benjamin, and they might all be punished for cheating the Governor.

"I have lost one son already," Jacob said. "You can't take Benjamin."

"I will bring Benjamin back to you," Judah promised.

"No," said Jacob.

But the famine grew worse, and in the end they had to go back, taking Benjamin with them. Jacob didn't want to let Benjamin go, but the brothers persuaded him. They took with them the best spices they had, and twice as much money as before, to try to prove that they had not been cheating the Governor.

Joseph had another test prepared for them.

He let Simeon and Benjamin go but he had a silver cup put secretly in the top of Benjamin's sack. The brothers started for home, and Joseph's servant came after them and accused Benjamin of stealing the cup.

Benjamin was arrested, and taken back to Egypt.

"We can't go without Benjamin. It would break our father's heart," the brothers said, and they hurried back to plead with the Governor.

It was Judah, the brother who had been responsible for selling Joseph into slavery, who plucked up his courage and spoke. He confessed everything to the Governor.

"We sold our brother into slavery, and told our father he had been killed. Our father was heartbroken. Now I have promised to bring Benjamin back to him. I cannot bear to see my father suffer again as I caused him to suffer before. I will stay here as your slave in Benjamin's place."

Judah and the brothers had changed, and Joseph knew they were truly sorry for what they had done to him. Their deeds showed it. Joseph kissed them and hugged them and told them who he was.

Joseph sent the brothers to bring his father and his family to Egypt, where there was plenty of food.

That was why God had arranged for Joseph to go to Egypt in the first place, so that the Children of Israel would be saved from the famine.

They all left Canaan, the Promised Land, just as God had said they would, but in time they would return.

That was God's promise to them.

Jacob saw his son Joseph again, and the brothers became the leaders of their own tribes, the twelve tribes of Israel.

A long time later Jacob died, and later still so did Joseph. The People of God were in exile, and they became the slaves of the Egyptians, which was what God had told Abraham would happen, but God still loved His people, and He sent another man to guide them.

The man's name was Moses.

He comes next.

Moses and the Bulrushes

oses nearly didn't live to be a guide and teacher of the Children of Israel. This is what happened.

Four hundred years had passed since the death of Joseph, and the People of God were still in Egypt. There were more and more of them, all over Egypt.

A new Egyptian Pharaoh had come to power, and he decided that something had to be done to keep these strangers in his land from taking over everything.

The Pharaoh made slaves of the Children of Israel, and put cruel slave masters over them, and did all he could to hurt them, but he still felt it wasn't enough. He was afraid they might grow too powerful and join with his enemies to fight against him.

Then the Pharaoh thought of a new plan.

It was simple, and very cruel. He decided to kill every boy born to God's people, sparing only the girl children. It sounds terrible, but that is what he decided.

Just after he decided it, Moses was born.

Moses' mother was proud and happy because she had given birth to such a beautiful, strong son. She wasn't going to let the Egyptians kill him.

So she hid him.

But you can hide a baby for only a short time. Moses began to grow bigger, and his mother knew that she would have to do something else. She didn't want to part with her son, but if she stayed in Egypt and kept him, he would be discovered by the Egyptians sooner or later, and they would kill him.

This is what she did . . .

First, she took a basket made of bulrushes and coated it with tar to make it watertight, so that it would float on water.

Then she took her little boy whom she loved so much and put him in the basket. She carried the basket down to the river at a place near the royal palace, and she set the basket floating on the water, with the baby in it.

That sounds like a terribly foolish thing to do to a baby, but it wasn't, because she had chosen a spot on the river where she knew the Pharaoh's daughter came every day to bathe.

Along came the Pharaoh's daughter, and she spotted the basket floating in the reeds. She sent one of her maids to fetch it, because she wanted to know what was inside it. You don't often find a carefully closed basket floating around on your favorite part of the river, even if you are a princess.

The Princess opened the basket.

The baby was startled and began to cry.

"Poor little thing," the Princess said, and she lifted him up and cradled him in her arms.

"That's a Jewish boy," somebody said. "Better kill it!"

"Kill him?" the Princess said, gazing down at the baby.

"That's what the Pharaoh ordered," the somebody said. "Kill it!"

"Nobody is going to kill him," the Princess said fiercely.

"Well, *you* can't keep it, can you?" the somebody said. "You know how the Pharaoh feels about the Jews."

That stumped the Princess. She knew she couldn't keep the child herself, but she couldn't hand a little baby over to be killed.

Up popped Moses' sister, who had been hiding nearby.

She didn't tell the Princess who she was, but she did come up with a helpful suggestion.

"I know a woman who would look after that baby for you, if you want to save his life," Moses' sister said casually, as if it didn't matter to her one way or the other. (It was true. She did know a woman! She didn't say that the woman she knew just happened to be the child's real mother.)

"It's a good thing you came along," said the Princess, and she sent for Moses' mother and asked her to care for the baby, who would have the Princess's royal protection.

The Princess gave the baby the name Moses because Moses means "drawn out," and she had drawn him out of the water. When the baby had grown a little more, the Princess adopted him, and he was brought up as a prince in the Pharaoh's palace.

That is how God saved Moses' life.

Moses and the Burning Bush

oses grew up in the Pharaoh's palace as a prince. Then he got into trouble trying to save a Jewish slave from the cruelty of one of the Egyptian slavedrivers. Moses escaped from Egypt and went to Midian, where he thought he would be safe from the cruel Pharaoh. There he married a woman called Zipporah, the daughter of Jethro.

One day, Moses was looking after Jethro's sheep on the slopes of a mountain.

He saw smoke and flames burst out of a bush on the mountain. The bush was burning, yet it *wasn't* burning: the bush was full of flames, but it stayed the same.

Moses went to take a closer look, and a voice said, "Moses! Moses!"

"Here I am," said Moses, looking around nervously. He didn't believe the voice could be coming from the bush, but it was.

"Don't come any closer!" said the bush. "And take off your sandals, because you are standing on holy ground. I am the God of Abraham, Isaac, and Jacob."

Moses was scared. Who wouldn't be, with God speaking to them out of a burning bush? Moses hid his face. He was afraid to look at God.

God said, "I am sending you to the Pharaoh so that you can lead My people out of Egypt back to the Promised Land of Canaan."

Moses was amazed.

It isn't every day this kind of thing happens to a shepherd out herding his sheep!

"I'm just a nobody," he said. "How can I go to the

Pharaoh and persuade him to let the people go?"

God said, "I will be with you. When you lead the people out of Egypt, you must bring them here and worship Me."

"The people won't believe me," Moses said. "What shall I do if they say that You did not appear to me?"

"What are you holding?" God asked.

"A stick," Moses said.

"Throw it down on the ground," God said.

Moses did.

The stick turned into a snake, wriggling about on the ground, and Moses ran away from it.

"Pick it up by the tail," God said.

Moses trusted God, so he tiptoed back and picked the snake up by the tail. It turned right back into a stick!

But Moses still wasn't sure.

"Put your hand inside your robe," God said.

Moses did, and when he took it out again, it was all scabby and diseased and covered with white spots.

"Put it in again!" God said.

Moses did, and when he took it out a second time, his hand was healed.

"That's two miracles," God said. "If you show them

those two, and they still don't believe you, take some water from the river and pour it on the ground. The water will turn to blood."

Three miracles should be enough for anybody, but Moses still didn't see how he could manage to convince his own people *and* the Egyptian Pharaoh that God had appeared to him.

Moses said: "No, Lord, don't send me! I have never been a good talker. I couldn't manage all the arguments there will be."

"Who gives man his mouth?" God said. "Who makes him deaf or dumb? Who gives him sight or makes him blind? I do! I will help you to speak, and I will tell you what to say."

"Please send somebody else," Moses pleaded.

God was angry with Moses, and his fears.

"Take your brother Aaron with you," he said. "He can do the talking and you can do the miracles."

And that's what happened.

It took a long time, and many terrible things happened, but in the end Moses and Aaron did what God had commanded. With God's help, Moses and Aaron convinced the Pharaoh that he had to let his slaves go.

The People of God set out for the land that He had promised Abraham many years before, but they weren't finished with the wicked Pharaoh.

He changed his mind and chased after them.

That's the next story.

The People of God in the Desert

oses and Aaron led their people into the desert, but no sooner had they gone than the Egyptians started grumbling about losing their slaves, and having no one to do the work for them.

"We'll go and get them back!" decided the Pharaoh. He called for his war chariots, and the Egyptians charged into the desert to bring the Children of Israel back into slavery.

God sent a pillar of cloud to lead the people through the wilderness, and at night it became a pillar of fire, so they could see where they were going and didn't have to stop. But the Pharaoh and his chariots were catching up with them, and despite all that Moses and Aaron had done, the people still did not have faith that God would save them. They were afraid.

"Did you have to bring us all this way just to die?" they asked Moses. "We told you this would happen! We would have been better off as slaves than dying in the desert."

"Don't be afraid," Moses said. "God will look after you. Wait and see what happens."

This is what God did . . .

Night was coming, and God moved the pillar back so that it lay between His people and the Egyptians. God made it as dark as night on the Egyptian side, but light as day on the other side.

The Children of Israel came to the Red Sea. They were trapped. They couldn't get across, and the Egyptians were going to catch them.

"Lift up your stick and hold it over the sea," God told Moses.

Moses did.

A huge wind blew. It blew all night long and drove the water apart, leaving walls of water on either side, but a stretch of land in between that the people could use to walk over to the far side.

The Egyptians charged on after them in the darkness. Dawn came and they realized they were in the middle of the Red Sea with walls of water on either side of them.

"Let's get out of here! God is fighting for the Israelites against us!" they shouted.

"Hold out your hand over the sea," God told Moses.

Moses did.

WHOOOOOSH!

One minute there was an army of Egyptians standing on a dry path, and the next minute the water came rushing back, and they were all drowned.

This time the Children of Israel were really free, but they were still in a desert, and a desert isn't a good place to be.

They came to a place where the water was bitter, but God showed Moses how to make it good to drink, and they were saved.

Then they ran out of meat and bread, and the people complained to Moses and Aaron about it.

"We wish God had killed us in Egypt," they said. "At least there we had food. You have brought us into this desert to starve to death." Despite all the miracles God had done for them, they still had little faith.

"If you complain about what we have done, you are complaining about what God has done," Moses said. "We are only carrying out His orders. This evening you will know that it was God who sent you here, not us."

41

All the people gathered together. Suddenly God appeared in a dazzling light, shining out of a cloud.

God said to Moses, "I have heard the complaints of the Israelites. Tell them that at twilight they will have meat to eat, and in the morning they will have all the bread they want. Then they will know that I am the Lord, their God."

It was easy enough to say that, but how do you make meat and bread in the middle of a desert? The Israelites doubted God, but they shouldn't have, because He did it.

That evening, at twilight, a whole flock of small birds called quail flew in, enough to cover the camp. There were birds everywhere. Meat enough for everyone!

That was the meat, but what about the bread?

They woke up in the morning.

No bread!

There was a lot of dew on the ground, but not a slice of bread.

They started grumbling again. They were a grumbly group, but they were in the desert, and terrible things had happened to them, so I suppose it is understandable.

The dew started to dry up, and when it dried it left a thin, crumbly stuff, like dry frost on the ground.

"What is it?" the grumblers said. "It doesn't look like bread to us."

Moses said, "This is the bread the Lord has given you to eat. The Lord has commanded that each of you is to gather only as much as you need."

They did, but some of them still didn't trust God, and gathered more than they needed. They ate some of the strange bread and they put the rest away, in case there would be no bread the next day.

The next morning the extra bread they had gathered had rotted.

Moses was angry with them, because they had disobeyed and gathered more than they needed, as if God wouldn't provide for them, when He had said that He would.

They didn't do it again. They gathered only what they needed, which pleased God, and Moses.

It was nice bread. It tasted like cookies made with honey. They called the funny bread *manna*, which in their language sounds like the word for "what-is-it?" They went on living on "what-is-it?" for years!

The Israelites should have been grateful to God, but instead they started complaining again.

"No water!" the grumblers and the doubters said. "Give us water to drink."

"Why are you complaining?" Moses asked. "Why do you keep doubting, and putting God to the test?"

"Why did you bring us out of Egypt?" the grumblers moaned. "To kill us and our children and our cattle with thirst?"

"What can I do with these grumblers?" Moses asked God.

"Take some of them with you, and go to a rock that I will show you," God said. "Take along the stick you used before. Bang it on the rock, and water will flow out."

It did!

There was enough for everybody again, which just went to show the grumblers and the doubters how wrong they were not to trust God.

At last they got through the desert to Mount Sinai,

where God had told Moses to bring them.

There God gave the people His Commandments to teach them about the way they were to live, and how they were to worship Him. God's Commandments and His promises are known as His Covenant. He told them to carry with them a written record of His Covenant in a special box, called an Ark. The Ark of the Covenant was to be always with them, as a sign that He was always present in their lives.

You will find God's Commandments and all His promises to His people in the Scriptures.

God loved His people. That is why He made His Covenant with them.

When they were wicked and turned against Him, God was sad. When they were foolish and doubted Him, God was merciful. When they kept their trust in Him, God was happy.

God kept His promise to the Children of Israel and brought them back to the Promised Land.

That is the next story.

Joshua and the Promised Land

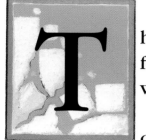he Children of Israel wandered in the desert for many years before God's promise to them was fulfilled.

Moses died, and a man called Joshua was chosen by God to guide the people. At long last Joshua led them into the Promised Land.

It wasn't easy.

First they came to the river Jordan, which was too wide and deep for them to cross, and they didn't know what to do.

God drew back the waters, just as he had drawn back the waters of the Red Sea for Moses, and the people were able to cross the river.

Then they came to a great city, called Jericho.

It had huge walls, and was filled with people who didn't want to let the Israelites in. The people of Jericho barred the great gates of the city against Joshua, and he didn't know how to get in.

So God told him!

Day one, they marched around outside the city walls, carrying the Ark of the Covenant and blowing their trumpets.

The people inside thought this was strange, because marching around blowing trumpets is not the way people usually go about capturing a city.

Day two, they did it again.

The people inside were getting puzzled.

Day three, more marching and trumpets.

"Let them!" said the people inside. "Silly idiots!"

Day four, the same thing.

"They're crazy, those Israelites," muttered the people

inside. "Really mad."

Day five . . .

"At it again," said the people in the city. "Don't they know how to fight?"

Day six . . .

"Don't take any notice. It's only the Israelites out marching again. Left-right, left-right, left-right!"

Day seven . . .

Day seven was different!

Joshua and his soldiers marched around the city with the Ark of the Covenant seven times, blowing their trumpets. Then . . . one long trumpet blast!

"What are they doing now?" asked the people inside the city. "They're all shouting. Don't they know that's no way to storm a city . . . ? *Help!* What's happening? *Oh!*"

The walls of the city fell down and the Children of Israel

charged in and captured the city!

God had kept His promise to them, but they didn't keep their promise to Him. They went on to many more victories, but they were always fighting and quarrelling.

God did not desert them, but their disobedience led to many troubles. The Promised Land was invaded by other people, and many of the new people worshipped other gods.

There came a time when the Philistines invaded the Promised Land and conquered the Israelites. The Israelites had forgotten their Covenant with God and I think God used the Philistines as a way of reminding them of it, and drawing them back to Him. The Philistines ruled over them for forty years, and then a boy named Samson was born.

The next story is his story.

Samson and Delilah

amson was strong. God had given him great strength, to help him stand up for his people against the Philistines. He fought the Philistines again and again, but this led to more trouble for the Israelites.

The people went to Samson. "You've gotten us into trouble with the Philistines," they said. "It is all your fault that we are being attacked, and we are going to tie you up and hand you over to them."

That's what they did, but they had forgotten Samson's great strength.

There were three thousand Philistines surrounding Samson, who was bound up with good strong new ropes.

Samson broke the strong ropes as if they were threads. He had nothing to fight with, but he picked up an old piece of bone from the ground (it was the jawbone of an ass) and . . . all on his own Samson attacked the three thousand Philistines.

He killed a thousand of them, and the rest ran away.

Another time, the Philistines caught Samson in the city of Gaza. He was inside, and they closed the great gates of the city to trap him.

Samson pulled up the gates, big doorposts, locks, and all, and he walked off carrying the gates on his shoulders!

But the Philistines caught him in the end.

They did it by using a woman he was in love with, named Delilah. They gave her eleven hundred pieces of silver to find out the secret of Samson's strength.

"If someone wanted to tie you up and make you helpless, how would he do it?" Delilah asked Samson.

Samson said: "Tie me up with seven new bowstrings.

That ought to do it."

Delilah tied him. Then she shouted: "Samson! The Philistines are coming!"

Samson broke the strings, as if they were cobwebs.

So Delilah knew that wasn't it.

She tried again.

This time Samson said, "Tie me up with ropes that have never been used."

She did.

"Samson! The Philistines are coming."

Within moments Samson was bouncing around the room, waiting to take on the Philistines.

"You're still making a fool of me, and it's not fair!" she said. "Tell me how to make you helpless."

"Try weaving a lock of my hair into a weaving loom," Samson said.

She did.

"Samson! The Philistines are coming!"

There was a crash, and Samson was free.

Delilah was very upset. She went on and on about it, which wouldn't have mattered if Samson hadn't loved her, but he did. In the end he gave in and told her the truth.

"My hair has never been cut," he said. "I made a vow to God that it never would be. If my hair was cut it would be a sign that I had lost my trust in God, and I would lose my strength."

Delilah cut Samson's hair while he was sleeping.

"Samson, the Philistines are coming!"

And this time the Philistines captured Samson. They were horribly cruel. They blinded him, and they chained him up with bronze chains, and they put him to work driving a mill like an ox.

They thought that was the end of Samson, but they were wrong.

One day they were having a great celebration in their temple, and they thought they would have fun and bring their old enemy out and tease him, now that he was weak and powerless and blind, and couldn't fight them.

They shouted: "Our god has given us victory over you!" and things like that.

Samson said, "Let me lean against the pillars of the building."

They probably thought that was funny too: the Great Strong Man having to lean against the pillars of the building, because he was so weak.

They were all dancing around Samson, shouting at him and teasing.

Samson prayed to God, "Give me my strength just once more!"

And God did.

Samson braced himself against the two middle pillars that held up the building.

The crowd thought that was even funnier.

"Ha! Ha! Ha! Look at the silly blind man, trying to pull down our temple!" they shouted.

The next moment, the pillars gave way, and the whole temple fell down on top of them. That stopped their laughter.

They were all killed, and so was poor Samson. He had trusted in God, and God had given him the strength to defeat his enemies.

The persecution of the People of God didn't end with

Samson, and the people began to lose faith. They wanted a king to lead them, like other nations had—a king who would make their laws and win their battles. Trusting in God wasn't enough for them anymore.

God was sad, but He sent them a man named Saul to be their king, and the tribes of Israel were united under him. Saul became a great warrior and led the people to many victories over their enemies, but he disobeyed God in many things.

Saul turned away from God, and so God chose a shepherd boy named David to guide the people.

How could a shepherd boy guide the people, when they already had a powerful warrior king?

That is the next story.

Saul and David

ing Saul was a troubled man, but when David played music on his lyre, the King felt better. David became a favorite of Saul's.

David was with Saul's army when the next big battle against the Philistines happened.

Well, it was supposed to happen, but it didn't.

It didn't, because the Philistines brought a great giant of a man with them, a man called Goliath. He marched out in front of the Philistine army and shouted at Saul's army.

"Choose a man to fight me! If he fights me and kills me, we will be your servants. If I kill him, then you will be our servants."

He was so huge that nobody wanted to fight him.

Nobody except little David.

"You can't fight him, David," Saul said. "He's too big!"

"God will help me," David said.

Nobody else wanted to fight Goliath, so Saul got David a big suit of armor and a bronze helmet and a coat of chain mail.

David put on all the armor, and took a big sword, but he was so small and the armor was so heavy that he couldn't move.

David realized what he had to do. He took off the armor and he got his staff and a sling, and five smooth stones from a brook.

"Are you sure about this?" Saul asked.

"God will help me," David said again.

Off he went.

Goliath, the huge Philistine, saw little David coming.

He nearly fell over laughing!

"What do you think you are doing?" he asked David.

"You can't fight me with that small staff. What do you think I am, a dog? I'll bash you and feed you to the birds!"

"God doesn't need swords and spears," David said. "God will help me win."

Goliath thought he was crazy. But then Goliath didn't believe in David's God.

"I'm going to kill you now!" Goliath yelled.

CLUNK!

David had fired his first shot. The stone hit Goliath on the head.

CRASH!

Over went Goliath!

David pulled out Goliath's sword and cut off his head. The Children of Israel cheered, and the Philistines all ran away.

Everybody was delighted. There was singing and dancing to welcome David back from beating the Philistines, and they started singing a new song.

"Saul has slain his thousands,
And David his ten thousands."

David hadn't really slain his ten thousands, but that's what they sang.

King Saul heard it, and he didn't like it. Who would—especially a king who was proud of being a fierce warrior?

"They'll want to make him King David next," Saul thought to himself, and he became very jealous of David.

David fought many battles in Saul's army, and won them.

Saul's jealousy grew worse and worse. At last he sent for his son Jonathan, who was a friend of David's.

"Kill David!" he said, but Jonathan wouldn't do it.

Saul had a try himself.

He threw a spear at David, when David was sitting playing his lyre, but he missed, and David got away. Then he sent murderers in the night, to kill David in his bed. But David wasn't in the bed. There was a dummy of David in the bed instead, and so David escaped again.

Saul kept trying to catch David and kill him, and Jonathan kept helping David. Several times David had the chance to kill Saul, but each time he spared the King. In the end it was the Philistines who killed King Saul, and so David became the new king, as God had wished him to be.

David was a good king. He ruled his people well, and defeated the Philistines, ending their rule over the People of God.

David had a son called Solomon.

The next story is all about him.

Solomon

Solomon was a great king, but the thing he is best remembered for is his wisdom.

This story is an example of Solomon's wisdom.

One day two women came to him with a very small baby.

The woman who was holding the baby said, "We both live in the same house, and we both had babies at the same time. That other woman's baby died, but mine didn't. Now she says this baby is hers, and mine died, but it isn't true."

"She's so upset by the death of her baby that she's out of her mind. That's my baby she's holding," the second woman said.

"No, it isn't, it's mine!"

"Yes, it is!"

They kept on arguing about whose baby it was.

"Bring me a sword," Solomon said.

That stopped them.

"What for?" they asked.

"Well, I've worked out what to do," said Solomon. "I have no way of knowing which of you is telling the truth, but I want to be absolutely fair."

"Ah, you're giving me the baby!" the first woman said, because she thought that would be fair. "You're going to give me the baby, and cut off that lying woman's head," and she laughed at the other woman.

"Oh, no, he's not," said the other woman. "He knows you are mad with grief at losing your child, and he's giving me the baby."

"Both wrong!" said Solomon. "I can't decide between

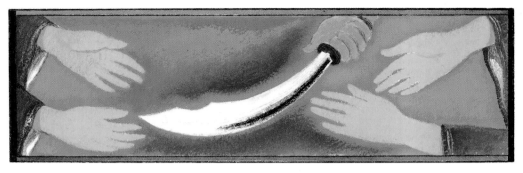

you, so I've decided to divide up the baby instead." He raised his sword. "Which half would you like?" he asked the first woman.

"Oh, no!" screamed the second woman. "Don't do that. Don't kill my baby. Let her have it instead."

"Dividing the baby up seems fair to me," said the first woman, who must really have been mad with grief.

Solomon had heard all that he needed to.

"It seems fair to you, because it isn't your baby," he told the first woman.

Solomon gave the baby to the second woman. She had proved she was the baby's mother.

That was the King's way of solving a very difficult problem.

Solomon was a wise king but even wise kings die, and after his death things got worse for the People of God. The kingdom which had been united under Saul divided again, this time into two kingdoms, Israel and Judah. They fought against each other and disobeyed God's Commandments, bringing all kinds of pain and suffering upon their people.

A long time later a king called Ahab came to the throne of Israel. He believed in another god, not the God of Moses, and God sent a man named Elijah to show him how wrong he was.

That's the next story.

Elijah

od sent Elijah to King Ahab to give him a message.

"In the name of the Lord, the living God of Israel, whom I serve, I tell you that there will be no dew or rain for the next two or three years until I say so," Elijah said.

"Bah! Don't believe in your God!" Ahab said. "Baal's the real god. I believe in him!"

Elijah went off and hid, which was very wise of him, considering the way kings went around killing off people in those days.

There was no rain for three years.

King Ahab had people out hunting for Elijah all over the kingdom, but they couldn't find him.

Then God sent Elijah to King Ahab again.

"There you are!" yelled the King. "The worst troublemaker in Israel!"

"You are the one who is disobeying God, and worshipping Baal," said Elijah.

"Baal's the real god!" said the King.

Elijah said they should test the gods.

The King agreed.

They brought 450 of Baal's prophets to a place called Mount Carmel to meet Elijah. Ordinary people turned up as well, hoping to see Elijah make a fool of himself.

"If the Lord is God," Elijah said, "worship Him. But if Baal is god, worship him instead. Go on. Choose!"

Nobody said anything.

"There's only one of me," said Elijah, "And there are 450 of Baal's prophets. We'll have a test. We'll kill a bull each. We'll each build a fire, and put the bulls on them, but we won't light the fires. Our gods must do that. The one who answers by sending fire . . . He is God!"

Everybody thought that was a good idea, but Elijah said the prophets of Baal should go first, because there were so many of them.

They killed their bull, cut it up, and laid it on the fire.

They started to dance about and pray to Baal, but nothing happened.

Elijah laughed at them. "Maybe your god is asleep!" he said. "Wake him up!" They prayed and danced again, but no fire came.

Then Elijah built his fire.

He made an altar, with a trench cut around it. He put the wood for the fire on the altar, and then he put the pieces of bull on it, and then he poured water over it all, so that the water poured down and wet the wood and filled up the trench.

"Ha! That wet wood won't burn," the people said.

But Elijah prayed to God.

And God sent fire down.

The fire was so hot that it dried up the water in the trench and burned up all the wood.

"The Lord is the one God!" all the people cried.

That was the end of the argument about who was the one true God.

"That's all very well," said King Ahab, "but where's the rain? Rain is what we need, you know. We've had three years without a drop."

"Go and have your dinner," Elijah said.

The King went away to have his dinner, and Elijah went up a mountain and prayed to God.

By the time the King had finished his dinner, Elijah's servant had spotted a small cloud, no bigger than a man's hand, coming up from the sea.

"Still no rain!" said the King. "Don't think much of your God!"

He rode off on his chariot and . . . it started raining and pouring, and the wind blew him all the way home. He was soaked to the skin, which served him right for not believing in God, after all Elijah had told him!

King Ahab's times were bad enough for the Children of Israel, but things got worse. Their land was conquered by the Babylonians, and many of them were captured, and carried out of the Promised Land.

The next story is of another man chosen by God to lead the people. The man was called Daniel.

Daniel

aniel was like Joseph. God had given him the power to understand dreams. When King Darius came to the throne in Babylon, he appointed Daniel as a supervisor to look after his interests, and Daniel was so good at the job that the King was thinking of putting him in charge of the whole empire.

The Babylonians didn't like that one bit. They kept trying to find a way to bring Daniel down, but Daniel was so honest in all his dealings that they couldn't find a way to do it.

Then one of them did.

"We'll use Daniel's faith in his God to trap him," he said.

Then they went to the King and said, "You are the King! You are the great King!"

"Yes, I am," said the King. Even kings like being told that they are great, and this one was no exception.

"Everyone who wants or needs anything in the kingdom should ask you to provide it," they said. "That is what great kings do. You make all the decisions."

"That's right," said the King. "I'm a great decider, I am."

"We're going to make a law that says so," they said. "It ought to be law, so that everyone will know how great you are. If people break the law by making requests of any god or man except you, they should be thrown to the lions."

"Just what they'd deserve!" said the King.

"You must make it part of the law that no one can change this law," the Babylonians said. "You are the King, after all, and we want everyone to know it."

"Sounds good to me!" said the King, feeling very

flattered, and he went ahead and made the law.

"We've got Daniel this time," muttered the Babylonians to themselves. They knew what would happen. All they had to do was wait.

Daniel was a good man.

Three times a day, every day, he went to his room and prayed to God to help him and guide him. Daniel prayed at the open window, facing the Promised Land, from which he had been taken.

He couldn't *not* do it.

Not doing it would have been denying God, so far as Daniel was concerned.

The Babylonians waited until they spotted him praying at the window and then they rushed off to the King with the news.

"Not Daniel!" he said.

"You made the law for everyone," they said.

"Well, I'll change the law," he said.

"You made the law so it couldn't be changed," they said.

"But . . ." said the King.

"No buts!" they said. "Throw him to the lions!"

The King was trapped, and so was Daniel.

"May your God, whom you serve so loyally, save you," said the King, gloomily.

"In you go!" cried the Babylonians, and they threw Daniel into the den with the lions. A large stone was placed over the entrance to the den, and King Darius sealed it with his own seal. The Babylonians sealed it with their seals as well, just to make sure.

"I feel really terrible about this," said the King, and he went back to the palace moping, and wouldn't be comforted.

First thing next morning, he rushed down to the den.

"Daniel, did your God save you?" he shouted, not very hopefully.

The Babylonians all stood around with big grins on their faces, waiting to pick up the bits of Daniel the lions had left over.

"Y-E-S!" came a voice from the den.

"Great!" cried the King, and he got Daniel out of the

den. There wasn't a single lion scratch on him, not to mention a bite.

"God sent His Angel to shut the mouths of the lions so they would not hurt me," Daniel said. "He did this because He knew that I was innocent, and because I have not wronged you, your Majesty."

The King thought for a while.

"Poor lions!" he said. "Nothing to eat all night! They must be ready for a snack."

And he threw the Babylonians who had plotted against Daniel into the pit.

And that was the end of the Babylonians.

But the King hadn't finished.

He sent a message around his kingdom that everyone should fear and respect Daniel's God.

"He is the living God, and He will rule forever!" the King proclaimed.

Daniel had remained true to the one God, and God had rewarded him, just as in time He rewarded the People of God, for Babylon was overthrown and they returned once more to the Promised Land.

God keeps His word, to those who trust in Him.

There is one last story I want to tell. It is about a man named Jonah, who was sent by God to the people of a city called Nineveh, which belonged to the enemies of the Children of Israel.

Jonah

here was a great city called Nineveh, where the people had fallen into evil ways. Nineveh belonged to people who were the enemies of the Israelites, but God cared for them too. He decided to send someone to tell them not to be bad.

He picked a man named Jonah.

"Go and tell them!" He said. "If they don't change their ways, I'll destroy the city and all the people in it."

Jonah knew God was giving the people of Nineveh a last chance, but he didn't want to go. He knew that God is merciful, and he didn't believe the city would be destroyed. Then he would look silly.

So instead of going to Nineveh, he went off in the other direction, and got on a ship going to Spain.

God wasn't pleased.

He sent a storm. It wasn't just any storm, but a real blast-and-gust one. The ship was tossed all over the sea, and looked as if it was going to break up. All the sailors were terrified.

"Let's draw lots and find out who is getting us into danger," they said, and they did, and guess whom they drew? Jonah!

"This is all your fault," they told Jonah. "Who are you, and what are you doing to bring all this trouble on us from God?"

"Well, I'm a believer in God, but I'm running away from Him," Jonah said miserably.

"You can't do that!" cried the sailors. "That's an awful thing to do. You got us into this, now you've got to get us out. What should we do?"

Jonah knew he was at fault for not obeying God, but he was a brave man.

"Throw me in the sea," he said. "I know I'm the cause of the storm, and if you do that, things will be all right."

They threw Jonah in the sea, and he sank, and all of a sudden the storm stopped, just like that. The waters became calm around the boat, so the sailors knew that what they had done was the will of God.

Down and down sank Jonah, right to the bottom of the ocean. He became all tangled up in seaweed, and then he was swallowed by a big fish!

It didn't bite him or hurt him. He found himself all covered in seaweed, floating around in the water in the big fish's belly, which must have been quite a shock for Jonah, not to mention for the fish.

Shocked or not, Jonah knew that God loved him. He praised God, right there in the wet, smelly darkness of the fish's belly, sloshing around in the water.

God heard him.

The fish swam toward land, and it threw up Jonah along with water and seaweed and whatever else was in its stomach at the time.

That left Jonah on the beach, all covered in seaweed, praising God.

"Don't just sit there!" God said. "I told you to go to Nineveh."

This time Jonah went, but he still had doubts.

"In forty days Nineveh will be destroyed!" Jonah told the people.

"Maybe, if we're all good from now on, God won't do it," the King of Nineveh said. "Everybody start praying."

They did, and they gave up their wicked behavior.

God was pleased, and decided not to destroy the city, which, of course, was just what Jonah had thought would happen.

"I knew this would happen!" he told God. "That's why I went to Spain instead of coming here in the first place. I *knew* you'd do that, because you are a loving and merciful God.

"What right have you to be angry?" God said.

Jonah stomped off into the desert, where he waited to see if anything would happen to the city.

Sitting around in a desert is hot work. Jonah made himself a shelter, but it wasn't much help. He was warm and sticky and full of grumbles.

God made a giant plant grow up over Jonah, to give him shade.

"That's much better," Jonah said to himself, but the next day God sent some worms to eat the plant, so it died.

"My plant! My lovely plant!" Jonah wailed, looking at the withered stalks where his plant had been.

"Are you feeling sorry about your plant dying?" God said. "What right do you have to be sorry?"

"Well, I am, and I think I have every right to be."

"Who grew the plant?" God said.

"You did," said Jonah.

"Right," said God. "You didn't grow it, you didn't do anything for it, and yet you feel sorry about its dying. Then how do you think I feel about Nineveh? I made Nineveh and the people in it and the animals. Just as you care for your plant, so I love the people of Nineveh. That is why I won't destroy them!"

God wants *everyone* to trust in Him.
That is the meaning of these stories.
There are many other stories in the Scriptures.
Read them, and try to understand them.
They belong to you.